For my parents

—S.E.B.

Copyright © 2010 by NordSüd Verlag AG, CH-8005 Zürich, Switzerland.
First published in Switzerland under the title *Oskar und Karotte*.
English translation copyright © 2010 by North-South Books Inc., New York 10001.
All rights reserved.
No part of this book may be reproduced or utilized in any form or by any means,
electronic or mechanical, including photo-copying, recording, or any information
storage and retrieval system, without permission in writing from the publisher.

First published in the United States, Great Britain, Canada, Australia,
and New Zealand in 2010 by North-South Books Inc., an imprint of
NordSüd Verlag AG, CH-8005 Zürich, Switzerland.
Distributed in the United States by North-South Books Inc., New York 10001.

Library of Congress Cataloging-in-Publication Data is available.
ISBN: 978-0-7358-2293-1 (trade edition)
Printed in Belgium by Proost N.V., B 2300 Turnhout, November 2009
1 3 5 7 9 • 10 8 6 4 2

www.northsouth.com

FSC
Mixed Sources
Product group from well-managed
forests and other controlled sources

Cert no. BV-COC-070303
www.fsc.org
© 1996 Forest Stewardship Council

Not far from his nest, Oscar met his friend Carrot.
"What an awful day!" said Carrot.
"Why is it awful?" asked Oscar, surprised. "Don't you want to play with me?"
But Carrot didn't want to play. She started to cry.

"What's the matter?" asked Oscar.
"Why are you so sad?"
Carrot wiped the tears from her eyes.
"It's Mommy and Daddy." She sniffed.

"Mommy shouted at Daddy. Then Daddy got mad . . . and Mommy got mad . . . and she was shouting at Daddy really loud . . . so Daddy ran out and slammed the door behind him." Carrot took a big breath.

"Then the whole house got really quiet. I don't think Mommy and Daddy love each other anymore. And they don't love me either."

Oscar listened carefully to Carrot.
"Don't be sad," he said. "Sometimes my parents fight
too. Most of the time I don't know what they're fighting

Oscar painted some squares on the ground.
"How about hopscotch?"
Carrot jumped up. "Great!" she said. "I'll
show you just how good I am at hopping!"

. . . Oscar started to fly instead of hop.

"That's cheating!" shouted Carrot. "If you're going to cheat, I'm not going to play with you anymore!"

Oscar and Carrot began to argue. Then Carrot started to sulk.

Oscar didn't know what to do. "Please don't be mad at me," he begged. "I only wanted to play."

But Carrot sulked and sulked.

Oscar looked around. "Look what I've found," he said. "The most beautiful four-leaf clover in the whole meadow."

Carrot looked at the clover. She thought about her mommy and daddy.

She wanted to tell them how much she loved them. But she also wanted them to know that she didn't like it when they argued.

What should she do?

Oscar had an idea. "Give them a present," he suggested. "A bunch of flowers for your daddy and a daisy chain for your mommy."

"Great idea!" Carrot cried. Suddenly she really wanted to get home.

Back home everything was quiet, but the whole house smelled like delicious dandelion soup.

"Aren't you arguing anymore?" asked Carrot carefully.

Mommy and Daddy winked at each other. "Did we argue?" they asked together.

"You sure did!" Carrot sighed.

Daddy gave Carrot a great big hug. "Don't be scared, little bunny! You know, all grown-ups argue from time to time. But when we argue, it doesn't mean we don't love each other anymore. And we love *you* all the time."

Daddy smiled. "What about you guys?" he asked. "Don't you ever argue?"

"Us?" Oscar said seriously. "Never!"
Then Oscar and Carrot burst out laughing.

Carrot wasn't worried anymore. She knew
her mommy and daddy still loved each other.
And they loved her too, and they always would.

"See," said Oscar.
"It was a good day after all!"